LIFE CYCLE OF A

SPIDER

By Kirsty Holmes

KidHaven PUBLISHING

LIFE CYCLES

PHOTO CREDITS

Front Cover & 1 – altstadtler, SKphotographer. 2–3 – dmitriyGo. 4–5 – Mix and Match Studio, MStoppello, Paul Hakimata Photography, rSnapshotPhotos, sebra, Shestakoff. 6–7 – Henrik Larsson, valleevalley. 8–9 – Marek Mierzejewski, Peter Yeeles. 10–11 – kurt_G, Tomatito. 12–13 – Nata Bene, Tyler Fox. 14–15 – Gwoeii, Wuttipat Jathutain, Eugene Kalenkovich, Sarah2, prambuwesas, microcosmos. 16–17 – Dirk Ercken, Cathy Keifer. 18–19 – 89studio, New Africa, Steve Collender, Tran The Ngoc, vector-map, Eric Isselee, Henrik Larsson, Moisieiev Igor. 20–21 – Tom Wurl, torook. 22–23 – dmvphotos, Eric Krouse, KF2017, Sarah2. All images are courtesy of Shutterstock.com, unless otherwise specified, with thanks to Getty Images, Thinkstock Photo, and iStockphoto.

Words that look like **this** can be found in the glossary on page 24.

Published in 2022 by
KidHaven Publishing, an Imprint of Greenhaven Publishing, LLC
29 E. 21st Street
New York, NY 10010

Edited by: Shalini Vallepur
Designed by: Brandon Mattless

Cataloging-in-Publication Data

Names: Holmes, Kristy.
Title: Life cycle of a spider / Kristy Holmes.
Description: New York : KidHaven Publishing, 2022. | Series: Life cycles | Includes glossary and index.
Identifiers: ISBN 9781534540026 (pbk.) | ISBN 9781534540040 (library bound) | ISBN 9781534540033 (6 pack) | ISBN 9781534540057 (ebook)
Subjects: LCSH: Spiders--Life cycles--Juvenile literature.
Classification: LCC QL458.4 H654 2022 | DDC 595.4'4--dc23

Printed in the United States of America

CPSIA compliance information: Batch #CWKH22: For further information contact Greenhaven Publishing LLC, New York, New York at 1-844-317-7404.

Please visit our website, www.greenhavenpublishing.com. For a free color catalog of all our high-quality books, call toll free 1-844-317-7404 or fax 1-844-317-7405.

CONTENTS

WHAT IS A LIFE CYCLE?

All living things have a life cycle. They are born, they grow bigger, and their bodies change.

When they are fully grown, they have **offspring** of their own. In the end, all living things die. This is the life cycle.

SUPER SPIDERS

Spiders are **arachnids**. They have tough **exoskeletons**, eight legs, and bodies that are split into two parts.

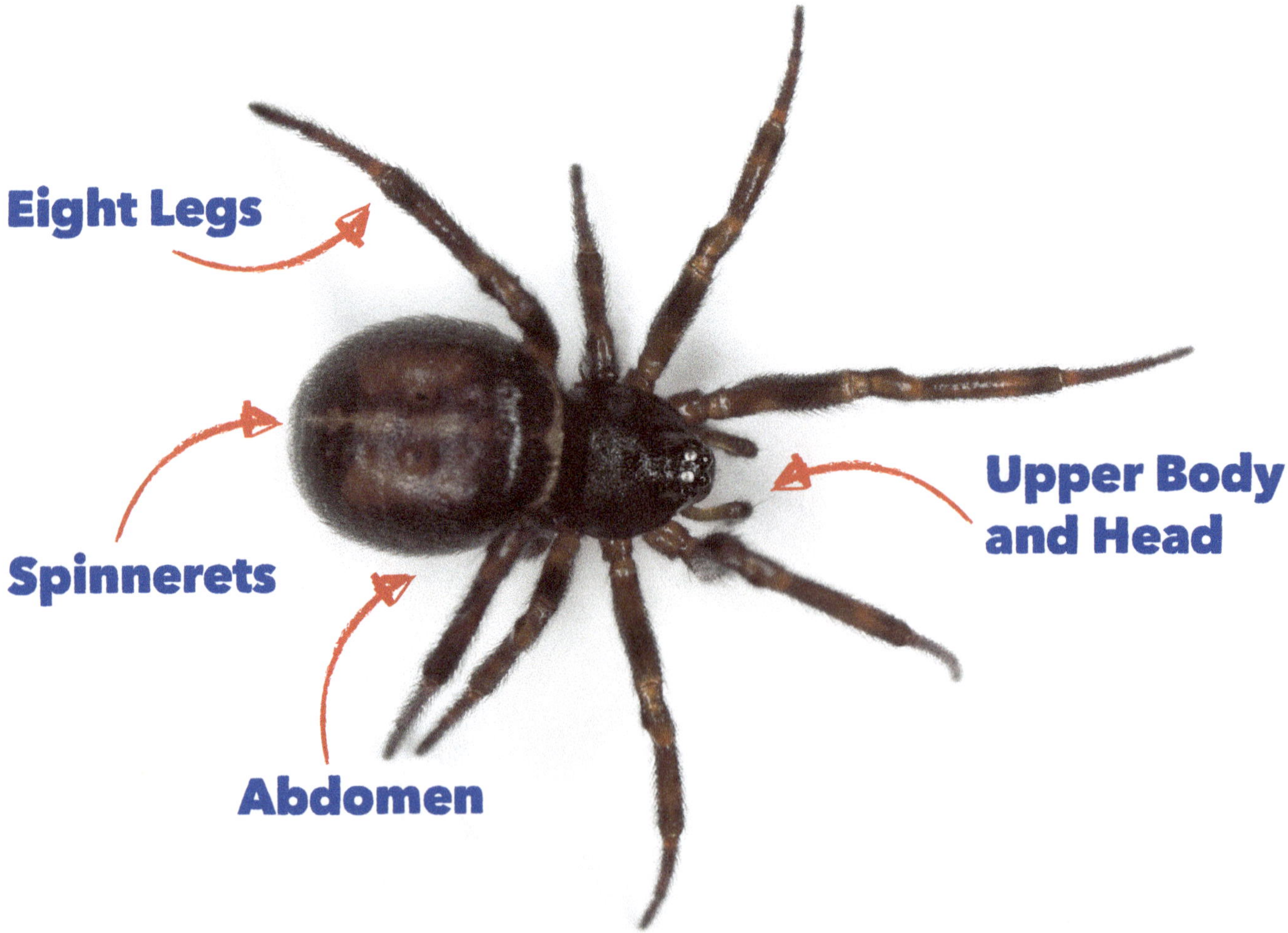

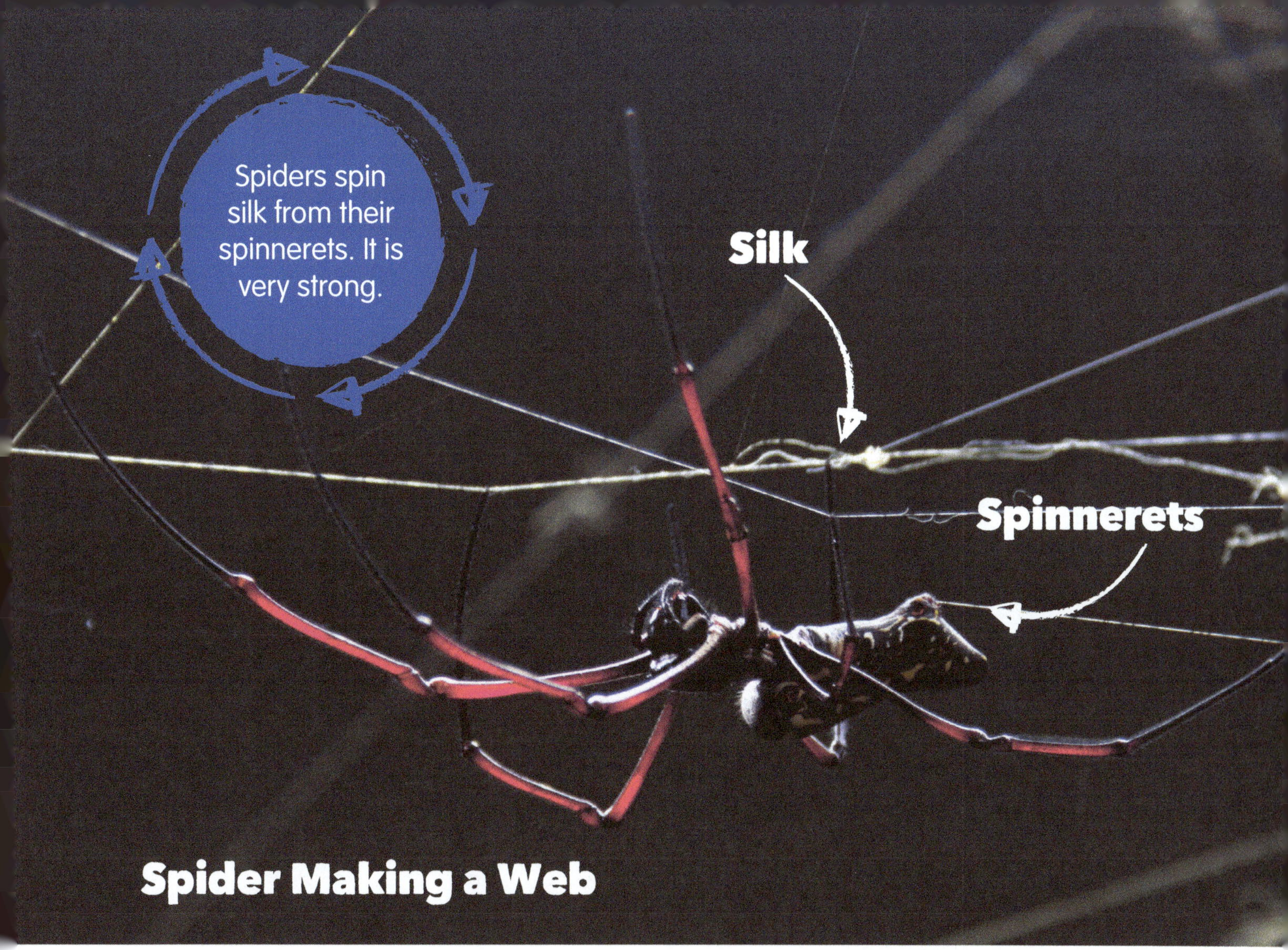

Spider Making a Web

Spiders live just about everywhere on Earth. Some may live in our homes, while others live in the wild. They make thin threads of silk which they use to make webs.

MAGIC MATES

Female spiders choose a **mate** carefully. Many types of spiders have courtship rituals. This is when the male spider must do special things for the female spider.

This tiny spider does a dance for a potential mate.

Female spiders are usually larger than males and can easily mistake the male for **prey**. It is thought that the male's courtship ritual shows the female that he is a mate, not a meal!

EXCELLENT EGGS

The female spider lays eggs and wraps them carefully in a sac to protect them. The sac is made from silk that is spun from her spinnerets.

Some spider mothers attach their egg sacs to a wall, plant, or web. Others will carry the egg sac on their back or attached to their spinnerets.

SURPRISING SPIDERLINGS

When the baby spiders hatch, they usually look like tiny copies of the parent spiders. Baby spiders are called spiderlings.

The wolf spider mother carries her spiderlings on her back.

Some spiderlings spin a little web and use it to fly into the air! This helps them travel away from their mother and find a place to live.

This is called ballooning.

SILKY SPIDERS!

Adult spiders are fully grown. They can spin their own webs. Each type of spider spins a different sort of web.

Spiders **molt** as they grow. When they reach their full size, they are ready to look for a mate and have babies of their own.

LIFE AS A SPIDER

This spider has caught a grasshopper in its web.

Spiders are carnivores. This means they only eat other animals. They are amazing **predators**. Most spiders catch their prey in their webs.

Some spiders do not use webs. Jumping spiders jump onto their prey. Spitting spiders trap prey in their sticky spit. Tarantulas hunt and catch their prey.

This large tarantula has caught a frog.

FUN FACTS ABOUT SPIDERS

- Spiders are not insects! Insects have six legs, and spiders have eight.

- Many spiders bite and can have a powerful **venom.**

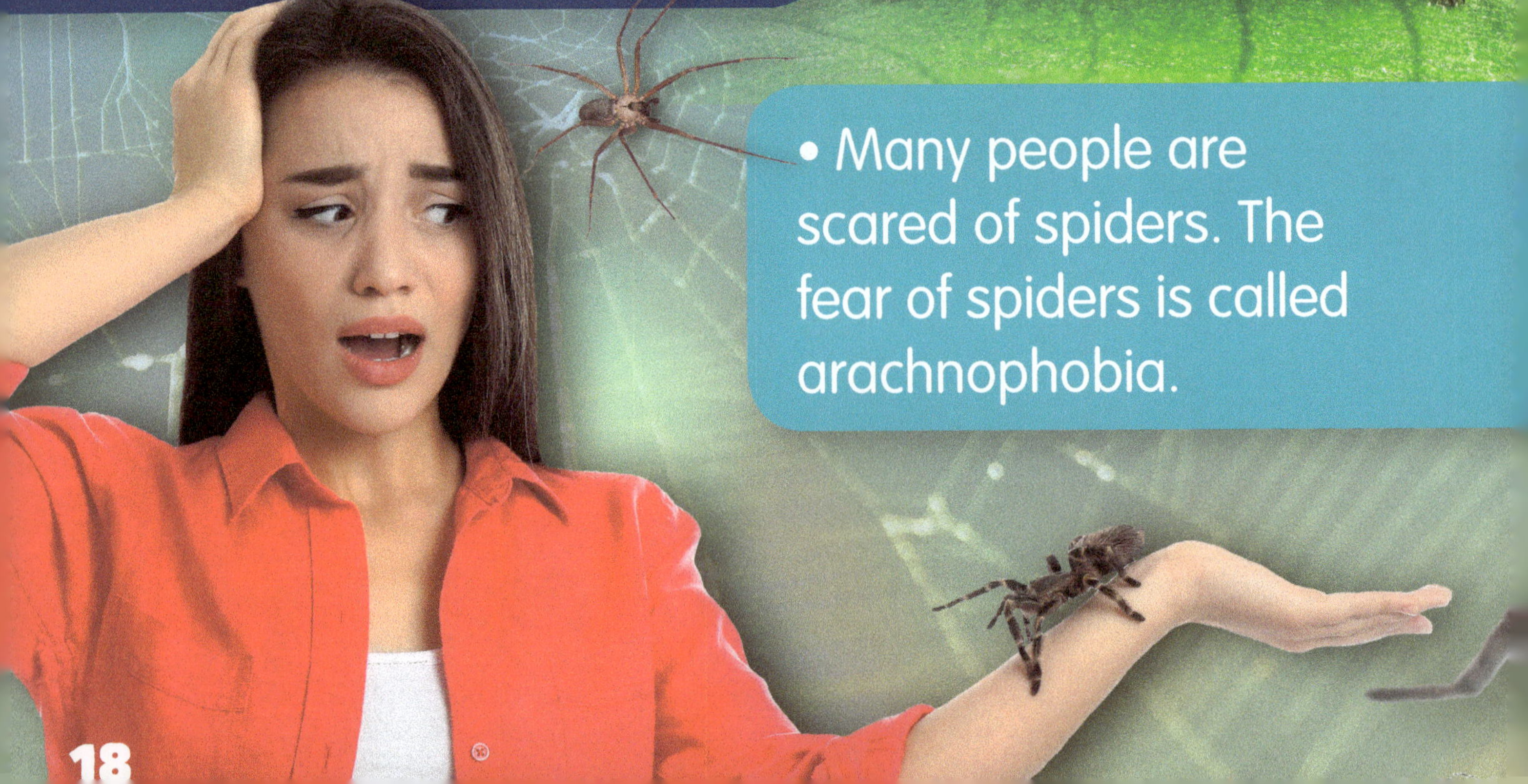

- Many people are scared of spiders. The fear of spiders is called arachnophobia.

• Spiders can be found on every **continent** except Antarctica.

• Some spiders, such as this peacock spider, are tiny...

... while others are huge!

THE END OF LIFE AS A SPIDER

The tarantula hawk is a wasp that eats spiders.

Many animals like to eat spiders. Lizards, fish, and birds are all predators that eat spiders.

Different types of spiders live for different amounts of time. Some spiders live for around three years, while bigger types can live much longer!

Larger spiders, such as tarantulas, can live for up to 30 years!

THE LIFE CYCLE

A spider's life cycle has different stages. Each stage looks different from the last.

The male spider finds a mate and performs courtship rituals. The female spins a sac for her eggs. The eggs hatch into spiderlings, which grow into adults, and the life cycle starts again.

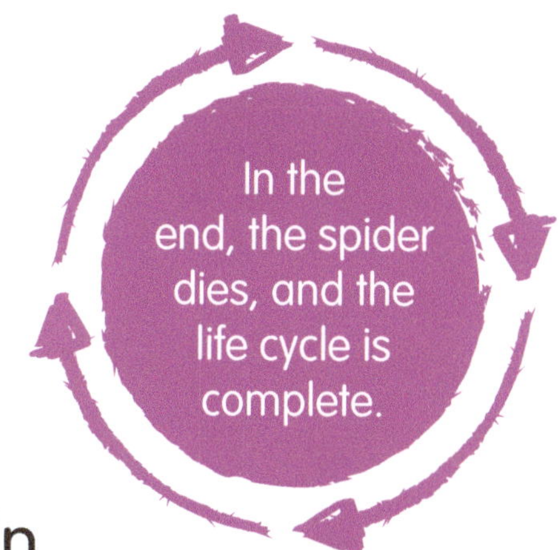

GLOSSARY

arachnids	animals that have eight legs, such as spiders and scorpions
continent	a large area of land, such as Africa or Europe, that is often made up of many countries
exoskeletons	the hard structures on the outside of some animals
mate	a partner (of the same species) that an animal can make babies with
molt	to shed a layer of skin, hair, feathers, or bone and grow a new covering
offspring	the babies of an animal or plant
predators	animals that hunt other animals for food
prey	animals that are hunted by other animals for food
venom	a harmful substance injected through a bite or sting

INDEX